BR

Ian Beck's
ALONE
in the
WOODS

A DAVID FICKLING BOOK

FOR

SCHOLASTIC
PRESS

For Lily.

Teddy Bears have such a quiet life,
don't they?

A David Fickling Book

Scholastic Children's Books,
Commonwealth House, 1-19 New Oxford Street,
London WC1A 1NU, UK
a division of Scholastic Ltd
London ~ New York ~ Toronto ~ Sydney ~ Auckland
Mexico City ~ New Delhi ~ Hong Kong

Published by Scholastic Ltd, 2000

Text and illustrations copyright © Ian Beck, 2000

ISBN: 0 590 54275 3 (Hardback) 0 439 99762 3 (Paperback)

Printed in China. All rights reserved

2 4 6 8 10 9 7 5 3 1

Ian Beck has asserted his moral right to be identified as the author and illustrator of this work
in accordance with the Copyright, Designs and Patents Act, 1988.

It was a perfect Spring day. "Come on," said
Lily. "I want to go on a picnic and fly my kite.
Let's ask Mum."

Lily asked if Teddy could come and, of course,
he could. So they gathered up the picnic things
and the kites, and set off.

Halfway up the steep hill, Lily asked, "Are we nearly there yet?"

"Not far," said Mum. "We'll be there soon."

At last they reached the top of Windy Hill.

They chose the perfect spot.

They laid out the cloth for the picnic.
Lily set Teddy down under a tree.

"Poor old Teddy," said Lily. "There's none for you, but you don't need a picnic, do you?"

After the picnic Mum said, "Let's fly
a kite. Which one shall we take?"
Lily chose the yellow one.

So Mum and Lily set off, leaving Teddy all
alone to guard the picnic.

Suddenly a great gust of wind blew, and
tugged at the red kite. The kite lifted,
and, oh dear, tugged at Teddy.

Teddy bump, bump, bumped along the ground.

He was lifted over some prickly brambles and just missed a cowpat.

As the kite lifted higher and higher, Teddy was dragged through a hedge backwards.

He held on to the kite string with all his might
because he was . . .

. . . flying! High up in the air. Now he was higher than the clouds.

He flew as high as an aeroplane.
"Whee!" waved Teddy.

Higher, higher and higher still, but this
was fun!

Then suddenly the wind dropped, and the kite
began to fall down through the clouds.

And Teddy fell with it, faster and faster, lower
and lower, down, down into the woods until . . .

. . . he landed 'plop', into something green and sticky! He heard voices whispering in the bushes.

When he looked up Teddy saw bright
eyes looking at him. He felt frightened.
Teddy was alone in the woods.

Then slowly, out of the shadows they stepped,
first one, then two, three, four, and then more,
and more, and more, Teddy Bears.

"You landed in our best jelly," they said.
"Never mind, don't be shy, tuck in, it's a
party, it's a . . ."

. . . Teddy Bears' picnic."
They feasted on jelly and honey buns and
lemonade, and then they all had a little sleep.

When Teddy woke up, it was getting late.
"How will I get back?" he said.
"Don't worry," said the bears, "we'll help."

And so they did. It took a little while to get Teddy into the air, after all the jelly and honey buns.

But after one big heave, the wind lifted him,
above the trees, over the hills, and far away,
all the way back, until . . .

. . . he landed, very gently, with the softest bump, just where he had started.

When Lily and Mum came back, Lily said,
"What a good Bear! You missed all the fun.
Never mind. Come on, time to go home."

Good Night, Lily. Kiss kiss.
And Good Night, Teddy. Sleep tight.
But we know what really happened, don't we?